BAT MAN ™ AND ROBIN THE TEEN WONDER ™

IN

THE CASE OF THE LAUGHING SPHINX

Story by Andrew Helfer
Illustrated by:
Ross Andru
Jim Aparo
Joe Orlando
Tatjana Wood

The full moon hung silently in the late night sky as a cool breeze swept through the grounds of the Gotham City Circus. The last show was over, and all the members of the circus were asleep. Even the animals rested peacefully. It had been a hard day for both man and beast, and all needed a good night's rest. But inside one tent a light still glowed brightly. Its occupant could not sleep. All he could do was sit and think and stare at the newspaper headlines.

Inside the tent, young Dick Grayson, a member of the acrobatic family called The Flying Graysons, knew his circus career was at an end. Earlier that day there had been a mysterious accident. In the middle of their act, Dick's parents had fallen from the trapeze and, suddenly, Dick was an orphan. Now he needed time to think about what he should do.

At first Dick did not hear the strange sounds coming from outside his tent. But when the lions began roaring angrily, he was startled. He turned to listen. There was a hissing noise like the sound of air being let out of a balloon. Then the other animals began howling and growling. Cautiously, Dick stood up and peered through the flap of his tent.

There were four men wearing gas masks. They had tanks strapped to their backs and were busy spraying the animals with some kind of gas. Their masks made their voices hard to hear, so Dick had to listen closely. What he heard shocked him.

WHEN WE FINISH SPRAYING THE ANIMALS WITH THIS GAS, THE ONLY THING THEY'LL DO AT SHOWTIME TOMORROW IS SLEEP!

YEAH...AFTER THAT TRAPEZE "ACCIDENT" AND THIS STUNT, THE CIRCUS OWNER WILL GIVE US ANYTHING WE WANT!

The more the young acrobat heard, the angrier he became.
These men were responsible for his parents' accident! They
were criminals, and they had to be brought to justice!

Fearlessly, Dick darted out of his tent, surprising the
sinister gang. Before they could stop him, Dick kicked one of
the criminals to the ground. His years of training on the
trapeze had made Dick strong and quick, and now he was
foiling the gang's scheme.

"You rats! You can't go around hurting people and animals!"
he shouted at the gang. But the odds were against Dick. It
was four against one, and the young acrobat needed help.

Suddenly, out of the darkness swooped... The Batman! The crooks were gripped with fear as the Dynamic Defender of the night descended upon them. Dick could see the anger blazing in the Caped Crusader's eyes and was thankful for his mysterious appearance.

IT'S TIME TO STOP YOU CRIMINALS ONCE AND FOR ALL!

BATMAN!

LET'S GET OUT OF HERE!

WOW! BATMAN! AM *I* GLAD *YOU* SHOWED UP!

"Four against one are bad odds in anyone's book, but I
think this will help even things up a bit," Batman said as he
landed a knockout punch to the leader's jaw.

"Go get 'em Batman!" shouted the courageous Dick
Grayson.

Without a pause,
Batman whipped his
Batarang at another
criminal, causing him to
slam into one of his
partners in crime. "I've
finally got the goods on
you 'gentlemen,' and
you'll all be going to
prison where you
belong!" Batman said.

Dick watched The Batman with admiration. The costumed
hero was as graceful as The Flying Graysons. But The Batman
was not there to entertain...He was fighting for justice!

Dick noticed one member of the gang sneaking up behind
Batman. With the grace of a gazelle, Dick jumped up,
somersaulting over Batman's shoulder, right into the
criminal's chest! Batman was amazed! He did not expect a
mere boy to be capable of performing such a feat!

A few minutes later the police arrived to arrest the four defeated criminals. Batman spoke to Dick, whose head was still spinning from all the excitement.

"Son, I've been tracking down that gang for a long time. They were wrecking circuses all over the country. When I heard about the trapeze accident last night I knew this gang was responsible. I'm sorry I arrived too late to save your parents, but I wouldn't have been able to round up these criminals at all without your help! The animals will rest all day tomorrow, but they'll be all right. What about *you*, Dick? What are *your* plans now?"

Despite his grief, Dick could hardly conceal the excitement in his voice.

"I wanted justice, Batman, and thanks to you, I got it. But now I'm all alone in the world. My parents are gone, but seeing you in action makes me want to spend the rest of my life fighting crime. Please Batman, could I help you?"

"All right son," Batman replied. "You deserve a chance after what you did tonight. I warn you, fighting crime is hard work, and you might not be cut out for it...But you'll have to decide that for yourself. Let's go!"

Within moments, The Batman and Dick Grayson were riding along the outskirts of Gotham City in the Turbo-powered Batmobile. As the cool night air swept by them, The Batman told Dick why he became a masked crimefighter.

"You know, Dick," Batman said, "I was an orphan too. Criminals were responsible for the death of my parents when I was just a boy. I swore then to devote my life to battling criminals wherever they may be. That's why I'm giving you this opportunity."

"I won't disappoint you, Batman," Dick answered.

Later, the two arrived at The Batcave, Batman's secret headquarters. All around them were the prizes and trophies he had gathered from years of crime fighting. "It's like a museum!" Dick said, fascinated by the amazing collection.

At this, Batman simply smiled and said, "You'll get the chance to look over everything in The Batcave a little later. Right now, and for the next few weeks, you'll be training physically and mentally for the life you've chosen. Let's get started!"

True to Batman's word, the next few weeks were painful and exhausting for the young Dick Grayson, but they were also wonderful. Dick fought off his fatigue to do all the exercises Batman was teaching him, and he accomplished them well.

The Batman, in his civilian identity of wealthy playboy Bruce Wayne, spent many hours training the young acrobat for the challenges Dick would face as a crimefighter.

"Gee, Bruce, we've already run five miles! Can't we take a rest?"

"Just one more mile to go, Dick. Then we'll see how well you do on the parallel bars!"

As the weeks passed, Dick could feel his body getting stronger and stronger. Each day he discovered muscles he never knew he had. Soon he could lift heavy sets of weights high over his head, where before he struggled simply getting them a few inches off the floor.

While Dick's body became stronger and faster, his brain became sharper. His eyes were able to follow the lightning-fast movements of the punching bag. In every respect, he was ready to work with his teacher in the war against crime. Dick knew the time had come when, at the end of a training session, Batman told him: "Now Gotham City will get its first look at a new, young crimefighter."

That night, Dick sat reading a magazine in the library of Wayne Manor. The article he read was so interesting that Dick did not hear Bruce Wayne enter the cozy room. Bruce held a costume in his hands.

"I think that you are ready to wear this costume," Bruce said. The only thing you need to decide is what name you will use in your crime fighting career!"

Dick walked over to a shelf and pulled out a book about Robin Hood, a brave man who fought injustice long ago.

"Ever since I was a little kid, Robin Hood has been my favorite hero," Dick said, "so I think I'll call myself... Robin!"

"I think that's a good choice," Bruce said. "Now it's time to try on your costume."

Moments later Dick returned to the room. In the shadowy light, Dick hardly looked like a young boy anymore. Instead, he seemed tall, strong, and ready for action!

After all these years of fighting crime by himself, The Batman had a partner. And with Robin The Boy Wonder by his side, Gotham City would be a safer place to live!

Days later, Bruce and Dick were sitting in the library when Alfred, the butler, walked in. Alfred was the only person who knew that Bruce and Dick were also The Batman and Robin.

"Excuse me, sirs," Alfred said. "The Batsignal is shining in the sky. You must be wanted at Police Headquarters."

In almost no time at all The Batman and Robin arrived at Gotham City Police Headquarters. Commissioner Gordon stood at the top of the stairs waiting for them.

"What seems to be the problem?" Batman said as he raced up the stairs.

"There's been a kidnapping, Batman, and frankly, I don't know what to do about it," Commissioner Gordon answered. He looked worried. "Come inside. I'll show you what information we have."

Inside Commissioner Gordon's office a slide machine projected a picture of an odd-looking man onto a screen.

"This is Frederick Smyth," Gordon explained. "He is a world-famous archeologist, and he is the man who was kidnapped. Smyth just made the greatest discovery of his career while in Egypt last month. He found this."

"This is the Laughing Sphinx," Gordon said solemnly, "and it is also missing. Hidden inside the Sphinx are three golden eggs. It's rumored that inside the eggs are the pieces of a map that will lead the owner to the greatest treasure ever imagined. Batman, you must find Smyth and the Sphinx before the eggs are smashed open and this great archeological treasure is destroyed."

"Have you got any clues?" The Batman asked.

"Only this. It was received in the mail this morning."

Batman read the clue.

He thought for a moment and said, "All right, Commissioner, we'll get on it right away. Robin, let's get back to the Batcave and feed this clue into the Bat-Computer."

You can't be an egghead to win at this game -- where questions mean prizes, and answers mean fame!

As the Dynamic Duo rode through the Gotham City streets, The Batman was silent for a long time. Then he said to Robin:

I'VE GOT A HUNCH THIS MAY BE THE TOUGHEST CASE WE'VE EVER FACED!

When the Caped Crusaders arrived at The Batcave, Batman headed straight to the gigantic Bat-Computer. Robin watched with interest as the Darknight Detective sat down at the keyboard to type his questions into the talking computer.

"I'm going to ask it which of our enemies could be responsible for this crime, and the machine ought to be able to tell us the name of the villain we should track down," Batman explained to the Boy Wonder. "In a few seconds we'll have our answer."

The Bat-Computer clicked and whirred. Lights blinked on and off. Suddenly, it spoke.

"There are four possible suspects in this case," the computer said in a cold, mechanical voice.

"Four?!" Robin said with surprise.

"Quiet, Robin," Batman said sternly. "Computer...continue transmission."

23

"Suspect Number One. The Penguin. Also known as Oswald Chesterfield Cobblepot. The Penguin uses umbrellas in his crimes. He is known for crimes involving birds. Since this case involves the theft of a Sphinx containing three *eggs,* he may be the culprit.

"Suspect Number Two. The Joker. Also known as the Clown Prince of Crime. This insane villain steals things that are of a funny, humorous, or comic nature. Since the stolen item is called The *Laughing* Sphinx, The Joker may be responsible for the crime.

"Suspect Number Three. The Catwoman. Alias Selina Kyle. Jewel thief, Cat-burglar, her crimes usually involve cats, both big and small. Since the Laughing Sphinx is half-cat and half-human, The Catwoman may be the guilty party.

"Suspect Number Four. The Riddler. Alias Edward Nigma. The Riddler's main characteristic is his uncontrollable need to outsmart The Batman by using perplexing clues. Since the clue received by Commissioner Gordon is, in fact, a riddle, The Riddler may be involved. However, this computer can offer no answer to the riddle itself. End transmission."

The computer clicked off.

"*Four* suspects! Wow! What do we do now, Batman?" Robin asked.

"Track down our first suspect, of course," Batman replied.

TO THE ICEBIRD ICECUBE FACTORY, ROBIN, IN SEARCH OF OUR FINE FEATHERED FIEND -- THE PENGUIN!

"The Icebird Icecube Factory! It looks more like a fortress than an icecube plant!" Robin said as he pointed to the dark building which stood on the outskirts of Gotham City like a mysterious castle.

"I've heard this place is The Penguin's hideout," The Batman said. "It's filled with all types of booby-traps to stop trespassers. We've got to be careful, Robin."

THE PENGUIN MAY BE WAITING FOR US!

Once inside the icy warehouse, the Dynamic Duo used their Bat-Flashes to find their way through the cold darkness. They searched through every inch of the frigid fortress but found no trace of The Penguin. Just as they were ready to give up, Robin spotted something.

"Batman! Through this trap door! I see a light down there!"

"Good work, Robin," Batman said as they both jumped through the hatch.

"LOOK!" Robin shouted as they landed. "An umbrella! That means The Penguin must be around here somewhere!"

"But before we go looking for *him*, let's investigate this clue," Batman said calmly.

When they walked through the lit doorway, Batman and Robin found themselves in a huge freezer room. Behind the umbrella left by The Penguin stood a huge mountain of perilously stacked icecubes.

"Careful, Robin," The Batman whispered. "The slightest noise might send those icecubes toppling down on us."

Without saying a word, Robin pointed at the umbrella lying in front of the icecube mountain. Batman knelt down and read the note pinned to it.

"Another riddle!" Batman whispered. "And it looks like The Penguin has flown the coop. We'd better track down our next suspect."

At that very moment, the Dynamic Duo were startled by the sudden appearance of none other than...The Penguin! The fowl fiend stood by the freezer door cackling hysterically.

"Ha! Ha! Ha! Looking for The Laughing Sphinx, eh, Batman? Well, you've come to the *wrong* place! The only thing you'll find here is a rather *icy* reception! Eck! Eck! Eck!"

With surprising speed, The Penguin turned to make his escape.

"Batman! He's getting away!"

"Stop him, Robin!"

"Robin! The sound of that door slamming! It's loud enough to make the icecube mountain..."

Batman's words were cut off by a rumbling sound as the icecubes began to crash all about the daring crimefighters.

"Batman! The Penguin's started an avalanche! We'll be buried alive!!" Robin shouted above the thunderous noise of the falling cubes of ice.

If they were going to escape The Penguin's frosty fix, Batman would have to think fast!

With astonishing speed, the Caped Crusader kicked loose one of the pipes lining the freezer wall, letting out a spray of ice-cold liquid nitrogen. Then, using his insulated gloves, he bent the pipe upward to face the falling cubes. The ice actually froze in mid-air, as the liquid nitrogen stopped the deadly cubes in their tracks.

Soon Batman and Robin were protected from the freezing avalanche by an umbrella of ice. This gave Batman the chance to get to a small charge of plastic explosive that he kept stored in one of the many compartments of his Utility Belt.

With a deafening roar, the explosive charge ripped the thick metal door off its hinges. When the smoke cleared, The Batman and Robin stood among the wreckage, ready for action.

"Come on, Batman, we've got to catch The Penguin!"

"Wait, Robin. The Penguin's long gone by now. He flew off, thinking we were finished. Right now, we should head for the Gotham City Amusement Park—I've got a feeling The Joker is up to no good there."

Flying high over the park, the Dynamic Duo noticed nothing unusual until Robin spotted a mob of people running in fear from the Tunnel of Love!

"Something's up!" Robin shouted to Batman. "People don't run out of the Tunnel of Love—unless there's something terribly wrong inside! Let's go down and investigate!"

When the Whirly-Bats landed, the Caped Crusaders leaped aboard one of the boats that floated through the Tunnel of Love. As the two crimefighters drifted into the ominous cavern, they could see only a dim light coming from far inside. The Boy Wonder shivered, but quickly overcame his fear and rode with The Batman down the peaceful stream that led to almost certain danger.

Inside the tunnel, the masked detectives saw what had caused all the fun-lovers to flee the peaceful amusement park ride in panic. Along the walls of the tunnel someone had placed life-like statues of creatures horrible enough to frighten even the bravest adventurer! Frankenstein, Dracula, The Wolfman, and The Mummy—all were leaning menacingly over the small boat as The Batman and Robin floated through the tunnel. It was a nightmare—but this couldn't be real, Robin thought.

Then suddenly, one of the monsters moved!

Robin shouted his warning to The Batman just as the monsters began to jump into the boat. Each monster had a look of hate in his eyes. All of them wanted to destroy the Dynamic Duo.

"Batman! We're sitting ducks!"

"Not if we fight back! It may be six against two—but remember—they're only human!"

"That takes care of two of them, Robin! We're doing just fine!"

"Tackling this mummy isn't easy—but I'll have him tied up in a second!"

"I hope you know how to swim, you reject from a horror show!"

"Save the joking for later, Robin! This is serious business!"

"This is no joke, Batman! That mummy *short-circuited* when he hit the water! These monsters aren't human—they're *robots*! And I think I know how to stop them! Just push them in the water!" Within moments, all that was left of the monsters were sputtering ripples in the calm water.

39

The dark tunnel was lit brightly by the sparks of the beaten robots.

"This type of sick humor has to be The Joker's work," Batman said.

From the corner of his eye, Robin spotted a thin figure heading for the tunnel exit.

"I think you're right, Batman," Robin said, "and there he goes! Let's get him!"

EXIT

Batman and Robin raced out of the tunnel, but it was already too late. By the time the two crimefighters got to the exit, The Joker was gone. But he left a clue. Robin spotted it first.

"Look! Floating in the water! It's a giant Joker playing card! I'll fish it out—maybe it can give us a lead in this case!"

On the other side of the card was yet another mysterious riddle. Robin read it aloud to Batman.

The man you seek is both here and there-- For on this night, he'll be on the air!

The Caped Crusader thought for a long moment after hearing the latest clue.

"Hmmm," he finally said. "We're getting closer to the solution. I can feel it. But we still need more answers." Suddenly, The Batman realized what he had to do next.

"Come on, Robin! To the Batmobile! We're going to the Gotham City Zoo to pay The Catwoman a little visit!"

At the Gotham City Zoo all was silent except for the footsteps of the Dynamic Duo as they ran towards the lion house. When they arrived there they found the outside cage *empty*! The lions were probably inside sleeping, Robin thought. But the *door* of the outside cage was *open*.

Inside the cage was a lion tamer's chair and a bullwhip. On the chair was a large sheet of paper with a riddle written in a now-familiar handwriting. Batman and Robin walked inside the cage to inspect the clue. Robin read it aloud.

To find the man who's causing you grief, turn on the tube, and get some relief!

"What does it mean, Batman?" Robin asked.

"Just a moment, Robin. All the clues are starting to fit into place. Let me see..."

As the Dynamic Duo thought about their latest clue, they did not notice The Catwoman quietly slinking up behind them. Quickly, she grabbed the cage door and slammed it shut with a loud clang. The Batman and Robin were caught totally by surprise.

"Ah…this is *purrfect*," The Catwoman gloated. "The famous Batman and Robin…behind bars at last!"

Batman pulled and tugged at the cage bars, but they would not budge. He and the Boy Wonder were trapped.

"I've got a little friend of mine waiting on the other side of those bars behind you," The Catwoman purred. "I'm afraid he missed his supper last night, so you can imagine how much he's dying to *meet*—or is that *eat*—you two? I *do* hope you all get to know each other *very well*! Ta-ta Dynamic Dumbos!" The Catwoman said as she crept back into the darkness.

Slowly, the cage door *behind* the Dynamic Duo opened. And then, out of the darkness jumped a gigantic, ferocious lion! Eyes ablaze, fangs and claws exposed, the hungry king of the jungle sprang at the startled Batman. Never before had the Darknight Detective faced such a savage opponent. The Batman was stunned, and although he tried to move out of the lion's path, the starving beast was too fast. In seconds, it was upon him, scratching and clawing at The Batman's costume.

"Robin!...I'm pinned down...Can't move...Can't get to my Utility Belt!"

"Hang on Batman! I'll get the situation under control!"

Like an experienced trainer, Robin grabbed the whip and began cracking it behind the lion. Then he gently pushed the chair against the lion's back. Angered by this interruption, the lion turned to battle the brave Boy Wonder, leaving The Batman behind.

Free to use his hands once again, Batman reached into his Utility Belt and tossed a sleeping gas capsule at the ferocious lion, just as it was about to pounce upon the Boy Wonder. Immediately, the big cat fell into a deep, peaceful sleep.

Robin cautiously stepped over the sleeping beast to aid The Batman as he picked the lock on the other side of the now-quiet cage.

"Thanks Robin," Batman said. "You saved my life!"

"No problem, Batman," Robin answered, smiling. "If you hadn't used that gas capsule when you did, I might have turned out to be dessert for our slumbering friend here!"

Once outside the cage, Batman returned to the task of fitting all the different clues together.

"The first clue mentioned a game—one that awarded prizes and fame for the correct responses. The clue at the icecube factory said that one player doesn't know the other's identity until the game is over. The Joker's clue said that the man we're looking for would be "on the air" tonight—that means television *or* radio.

But the last clue mentioned "tube"—which means tv. So when you put all the clues together they tell us that Frederick Smyth is going to be on a tv game show tonight!"

Robin snapped his fingers. He knew the solution!

"...And the only tv game show where contestants try to figure out people's occupations is ...*WHAT'S MY JOB?*'! Quick, Batman! To the television studio!"

As the Batmobile raced towards the Gotham City television station, Robin switched on the tv monitor built into the fantastic car's dashboard. "What's My Job?" was just beginning. The announcer was introducing the show and its host. Robin listened closely to the voice.

"Live from Gotham City—It's time for 'What's My Job?'! The weekly game show that asks the question—What do *you* do for a living? And now, here's the host of our show— Edward Nigma!!"

"Batman!" Robin shouted, hardly able to believe his ears and eyes. "Edward Nigma's not the host of 'What's My Job?'! Edward Nigma is..."

"Yes, I know, Robin," Batman answered calmly. "Nigma is...The Riddler. He's probably holding the entire staff of that tv station hostage so he can pull off this crazy stunt. Keep on listening—we've got to find out what his plan is."

"Good evening ladies and gentlemen. I'm Edward Nigma, your extra-special host for this edition of 'What's My Job?' Tonight we have a very special guest, because hidden among our four contestants is *Frederick Smyth*, the missing, world-famous archeologist!

"Is he hidden under the mask of Horus, the Egyptian Hawk God? Or Bubastes, the Cat? Or Anubus, the Jackal? Perhaps Amon, the Ram? Well, whichever it is, we'll find out, and when we do, Mr. Smyth will watch us crack open the three golden eggs of his Laughing Sphinx to show our nation-wide audience what treasures lay within!"

"To help determine which of our contestants is really Mr. Smyth, we have called upon the distinguished staff of McNulty's Pool Hall and Gymnasium to assist in our investigation. Gentlemen, you may begin your questioning ...It's time to play... 'WHAT'S MY JOB?' Hee! Hee! Hee!"

Robin stared, open-mouthed, at the small television screen. "Batman—that guy's really nuts!" he said.

"I'm not so sure, Robin," Batman answered. I've fought The Riddler before; he may be a little off the wall, but this kind of display seems more like the Joker's style. There's more to this than meets the eye." The Batman paused a moment, then added, "Turn the set off, Robin. I have a plan. If only we can get there in time!"

Twenty minutes later, "What's My Job?" was reaching its climax.

"Well, contestants," Edward Nigma cackled, "You've managed to stump our panel of...er... experts, so what else can I say except...IT'S TIME TO UNMASK!!"

At this cue, three contestants lifted off their masks to reveal themselves as...The Penguin, The Catwoman, and The Joker! Frederick Smyth, the fourth contestant, was tied up and gagged, so one of the panelists got up and pulled off his mask.

The audience was stunned by the sudden appearance of the villains.

"And now," Nigma continued, "since everyone else has revealed himself, I guess our television audience won't be *too* upset if their favorite game show host turns out to be none other than...The Riddler! Ladies and gentlemen, it's time for the highlight of our show... Let's crack open the eggs of...The Laughing Sphinx!"

The studio audience was horrified. Shocked, they sat glued to their seats, but each viewer hoped someone or something would put an end to the villains' evil plan.

Meanwhile the villains gloated as they prepared to smash the eggs.

   As if in answer to the audience's silent prayers, the
Dynamic Duo suddenly swept into view. Now, the four newly-
teamed villains were shocked, and could only stare up in
disbelief as the Caped Crusaders were thwarting their evil
scheme.
   "I thought you got *rid* of them!" said The Joker.
   "Awk! And I thought *you* did," answered The Penguin.
   "I thought *I* finished them off," said The Catwoman.
   "What does it matter?" groaned The Riddler. "We're *all*
done for!"

The audience shouted with glee as Robin smoothly swept by the four arguing villains, plucking up the Sphinx and its eggs as he passed.

"Sorry I've got to run, fellas," he shouted down at the flabbergasted villains, "but I've got to take my Sphinx for a walk!"

Meanwhile, near the ceiling of the television studio, Batman was planning the final downfall of the evil team. Seconds after The Boy Wonder made his television debut, Batman cut loose the final cable holding up the huge "What's My Job?" sign.

With a tremendous thud the sign crashed down around the villainous crew! The audience went wild!

"Give 'em one for me!"

"Clobber those crooks!"

"Knock their blocks off!"

Soon, the entire audience was chanting "BAT-MAN, BAT-MAN!!"

As Batman swung down to the stage on his Batrope, the audience rose to give him a standing ovation!

Then Robin returned to toss a final Batarang around the four beaten evil-doers. Batman smiled and waved at the cheering crowd. He was not used to being a television star, but he accepted the audience's cheers and applause graciously.

"Is everything O.K.?" he whispered to Robin.

"Everything's fine, Batman," Robin answered, grinning. "I untied Smyth and he led me to the rest of the crew. They were locked up backstage. The Sphinx is in safe hands once again!"

AWK! THIS IS THE LAST TIME I LISTEN TO YOUR CRAZY TEAM-UP IDEAS, JOKER!

THAT GOES DOUBLE FOR ME!

After the show was over, Commissioner Gordon arrived with the Police to take away the four criminals. Gordon was anxious to congratulate the Caped Crusaders.

"I got to the studio as soon as I could, but it looks like you fellows beat me to the punch!"

"You might say that," Robin smiled.

"Well," Gordon answered, "it was a great show, Dynamic Duo! I saw it all on TV along with millions of other viewers! Gotham City will sleep safely tonight because of you two!"

"Whew!" Robin said. "What a job!"

"It's all in a night's work," Batman answered. "You know, we did three things tonight, Robin. We rescued Frederick Smyth, and we saved The Laughing Sphinx from the clutches of four of our deadliest foes..."

"What's the third thing?" Robin asked.

"Well," Batman answered, a grin appearing on his face, "we probably made 'What's My Job?' the most popular game show in television history!"

"Oh brother," Robin groaned. "Let's go home, Batman."

"Robin, you just read my mind."